GREETINGS FROM SOMEWHERE

The Mystery of the Gold Coin

BY HARPER PARIS • ILLUSTRATED BY MARCOS CALO

LITTLE SIMON

New York London Toronto Sydney New Delhi

LITTLE SIMON
An imprint of Simon & Schuster Children's Publishing Division • 1230 Avenue of the Americas, New York, New York 10020 • Copyright © 2014 by Simon & Schuster, Inc. All rights reserved, including the right of reproduction in whole or in part in any form. LITTLE SIMON is a registered trademark of Simon & Schuster, Inc., and associated colophon is a trademark of Simon & Schuster, Inc. For information about special discounts for bulk purchases, please contact Simon & Schuster Special Sales at 1-866-506-1949 or business@simonandschuster.com. The Simon & Schuster Speakers Bureau can bring authors to your live event. For more information or to book an event contact the Simon & Schuster Speakers Bureau at 1-866-248-3049 or visit our website at www.simonspeakers.com. Designed by John Daly. Manufactured in the United States of America 1213 FFG First Edition 10 9 8 7 6 5 4 3 2 1
Library of Congress Cataloging-in-Publication Data
Paris, Harper. The mystery of the gold coin / by Harper Paris ; illustrated by Marcos Calo. – First edition. pages cm. – (Greetings from somewhere ; #1) Summary: Second graders Ethan and Ella are sad about moving away from their hometown to travel the world with their mom, a journalist, and dad, who will home school them, but before they go they have a mystery to solve. I. Calo, Marcos. II. Title. PZ7.P21748Mys 2014 [E]– dc23 2013006969
ISBN 978-1-4424-9718-4 (pbk)
ISBN 978-1-4424-9719-1 (hc)
ISBN 978-1-4424-9720-7 (eBook)

TABLE OF CONTENTS

CHAPTER 1

The Surprise

"So what's the surprise?" Ethan Briar asked.

"Yeah, what is it, Mom and Dad?" Ethan's twin sister, Ella, chimed in.

Their mother, Josephine, smiled nervously. Their father, Andy, reached over and squeezed her hand. Ella tried to guess what they were going to say. Was it going to be a new puppy? Or maybe cool matching bikes?

"Ta-da! We're moving," Mr. Briar announced.

"You mean to a new house?" Ella asked, confused.

Mrs. Briar shook her head. "No, not to a new house. I just accepted a new job. I'm going to be the travel writer for the *Brookeston Times*."

"So why do we have to move? The *Brookeston Times* is in Brookeston," Ella pointed out. The *Times* was their town's newspaper—everyone read it.

"That's the exciting part," Mr. Briar said. "Starting next week we'll be traveling to different foreign cities so your mom can write about them."

"Foreign, like, another country?" Ethan asked.

"Yes," Mr. Briar said happily. "Like Spain and England

and Peru and India and—"

"Wait! Did you say *next week?*" Ella interrupted.

"Yep. We're leaving next Sunday," Mrs. Briar said.

"Next Sunday?!" Ethan exclaimed. "What about school? And soccer?"

"And our friends? And Grandpa Harry? Will we be able to visit them?" Ella asked.

"Well . . . ," Mrs. Briar paused. "Not right away. But we can stay in touch

with everyone. And, of course, we'll come back to Brookeston—"

"Someday. We're just not yet sure when," Mr. Briar finished.

Silence.

Ethan put his fork down. Ella had lost her appetite, too.

"It'll be the adventure of a lifetime," Mr. Briar said brightly. "We'll see some of the most incredible sights in the world! Places like the Great Wall of China, the Eiffel Tower in France—"

"Do they have soccer in China and France?" Ethan cut in.

"Yes, of course! And as for school, we've already spoken to Principal McDermott. I'll be homeschooling you both," Mr. Briar went on.

Mr. Briar was a history professor at Brookeston University. He was supersmart. He knew stuff like who invented the boogie board (Tom Morey) and the name of the first king of England (Egbert).

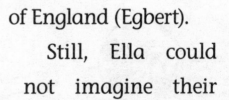

Still, Ella could not imagine their

dad being *their* teacher. He didn't sing silly "good morning" songs like their *real* second-grade teacher, Mrs. Applebaum. And he didn't serve green milk on St. Patrick's Day, either.

Mrs. Briar stood up. "Who wants dessert? Your dad picked up something special from Petunia Bakery to celebrate."

"I'm not hungry," Ella said quietly.

"Me neither. Can we go to the tree house?" Ethan asked.

Mrs. Briar cast a worried look at her husband. Ella and Ethan never turned down a treat from their very favorite bakery.

"Sure. We can just save you some dessert," Mr. Briar told them.

Ethan and Ella jumped up from the table and rushed out of the dining room.

Dessert was the last thing on their minds.

CHAPTER 2
Was It All a Dream?

The twins crossed the backyard to the old maple tree. The sky was deep blue with a sprinkling of stars. Crickets croaked in the distance. The air was cool and smelled like flowers.

They climbed the rope ladder up to the wooden tree house. Then they plopped down on the floor pillows.

"Worst. News. Ever," Ella declared.

"I don't get it. Mom already *has* a job with the *Brookeston Times*," Ethan said.

"This is a *different* job, though. She'll get to travel, just like Grandpa Harry did," Ella pointed out.

Grandpa Harry was their mom's dad. He was a famous archaeologist. That meant that he studied people from the ancient past by looking at buildings, artwork, and other things they left behind. When his wife, Grandma Lucy, was still alive, they used to travel all over the world for his work.

"Where are we going to live?" Ella wondered.

"How can we leave Brookeston? And our tree house? And our friends?" Ethan said.

Ella hugged her knees to her chest. "Hannah will probably find a new best friend while I'm gone."

"Yeah. Theo will probably find someone else to go to the comic-book store with," Ethan mumbled.

The twins grew quiet again. They had a million questions and worries swirling around in their heads—but no answers.

Ethan gazed up at a map of Brookeston on the tree house wall. Their school was just down the street from their house. Also nearby were some of their favorite spots: the playground, the duck pond, and the big fountain in the town square where they made wishes.

Next to the map of their town, the map of the world seemed so much bigger. And so much scarier . . .

"Hello?"

Someone was coming

up the rope ladder. A moment later, Mr. Briar's head appeared in the doorway.

"What's the password?!" the twins shouted at the same time.

"Um . . . uh . . . spaghetti and meat-balls?" Mr. Briar guessed.

"Wrong!" Ethan replied.

"I actually just came out here to get you guys. It's early bedtime tonight. Your mom wants us to spend the day tomorrow packing," Mr. Briar explained.

Ella looked at her brother. "Maybe when we wake up tomorrow, we'll realize this was just a dream," she said hopefully.

Ethan tried to smile. "Yeah, maybe."

CHAPTER 3

A Visitor!

Exactly one week later, Ella woke up with a start. It hadn't been a dream—the Briars were moving the next day. Ella barely recognized her bedroom. There were boxes everywhere. Boxes of books. Boxes of clothes. Boxes of toys and other things, like her seashell and shark teeth collections.

The Briars had spent much of the

past week sorting their belongings into two categories: stuff they would take with them on their trip around the world and stuff they would put away in the attic.

While they were gone, another family was going to rent the house. Ella tried to picture a strange kid taking over her room. What if he or she was a baby who covered Ella's desk with stickers? That desk was where Ella sat and wrote all her mystery stories—including her latest one, "The Case of the Missing Diamond."

Ella sighed and got out of bed.

The doorbell rang downstairs. A moment later Mrs. Briar yelled, "Ella! Ethan! There's someone here to see you!"

Ella went out into the hallway. She saw that Ethan's door was still closed. She used their secret knock: three quick knocks, a pause, and then three more

quick knocks. It was code for "hi."

"Ethan? Are you awake?" she called out.

"No," came the reply from inside.

Ella opened the door and went in. Ethan was in bed, buried under his soccer-ball sheets. His room was a maze of boxes.

"Mom says we have a visitor," Ella said.

"I'm sleeping," came Ethan's voice from under the sheets.

Ella glanced around. "You still have a lot of packing to do."

Ethan poked his head out. His wavy brown hair was sticking up. "That's part of my brilliant plan. I'm not going to finish packing. That way, we'll miss our plane tomorrow."

Ella considered this. "I don't think that'll work. Mom is really organized. She'll make you finish packing."

Ethan groaned.

"Come on, Ethan," Ella said.

Downstairs, their surprise guest was waiting for them in the living room.

"Grandpa Harry!" Ethan and Ella shouted. They rushed into his arms and gave him a big hug. Grandpa Harry lived in Fall Creek, which was the next town over. The twins saw him at least once a week.

"God morgon!" Grandpa Harry said merrily. He always greeted them in a different foreign language.

"Is that German?" Ethan guessed.

"Close. It's Swedish. Did I ever tell you kids about the time your grandmother and I stayed in a hotel in Sweden that was made entirely of ice?"

"Didn't it melt in the summer?" Ella asked.

"Didn't you and Grandma freeze?" Ethan piped up at the same time.

Grandpa Harry laughed. "They rebuilt the hotel every winter. And no, we didn't freeze. But enough about me. I hear you kids are starting your big adventure tomorrow!"

The twins stopped smiling.

GREETINGS FROM SWEDEN!

Grandpa Harry knelt down in front of them. "What's the matter, my dears?" he asked gently.

"We . . . we don't want to go," Ella confessed.

"I understand," Grandpa Harry said. "It's hard to leave everything you know behind. But guess what?"

"What?" Ella and Ethan asked.

"Life is all about adventures," Grandpa Harry replied. "And there is a whole world out there for you to discover. A world full of ice hotels, castles, ancient ruins . . . I could go on and on. Brookeston will always be

here, waiting for you. Your house will be here. *I'll be here.*"

The twins nodded slowly.

"Oh, I almost forgot!" Grandpa Harry reached into his jacket and pulled out two packages. "I have some *bon voyage* presents for you."

Ella knew that *bon voyage* meant "have a good trip!" in French. Her mom used to say that to Grandpa Harry and Grandma Lucy whenever they left for a new destination.

Ethan opened his present right away. Inside was a box containing an old-fashioned-looking gold coin. It had a picture of a globe on one side and a hawk on the other.

"Cool!" he said, grinning. "Thanks, Grandpa! What does the coin mean—"

But Ethan was interrupted by a gasp from Ella.

"Thank you, Grandpa Harry!" Ella

exclaimed. She had opened her present. It was a journal with a beautiful purple cover.

"I know how much you love to write, Ella," Grandpa Harry replied. "I thought you could use this to take notes on your travels. It might come in handy for solving mysteries, too."

"Solving mysteries?" Ella asked.

"What do you mean?" Ethan piped up curiously.

Grandpa Harry winked at the kids. "I've learned that when you start a big adventure, you never know when a mystery might land in your path."

CHAPTER 4

The Missing Coin
on Moving Day

"We have to be at the airport at four p.m.," Mrs. Briar said over Sunday brunch the next day. "Our taxi will be here at three to pick us up."

Ethan glanced at his watch. It was almost noon.

They were having a farewell brunch with Grandpa Harry. Mr. Briar had made pancakes. Grandpa Harry had brought strawberries from a nearby farmers' market.

"Let's figure out our schedules for the next few hours," Mrs. Briar went on. "I have to pick up some last-minute things at the mall. Andy, can you finish up the cleaning? And, Dad, can you supervise the kids? I made a to-do list for them."

Uh-oh, Ethan thought. *One of Mom's famous to-do lists.*

"I'd be glad to help them," Grandpa Harry said.

Mrs. Briar handed the to-do list to Ethan and Ella. It was about a mile long. Ethan felt dizzy just reading the

TO DO

-Pack your backpacks with activities for the plane.

-Check your closets and make sure they're empty.

-Ditto dresser drawers

-Ditto bookshelves

-Ditto under your beds

-Ditto the basement playroom

-Tape up all boxes labeled with your names.

list. How were they going to get all this done?

Mr. Briar began clearing the dishes. Brunch was over. The day was flying by. Ethan wasn't ready to get up and go.

He dug into the pockets of his Brookeston Boomers hoodie. "Oh, no!" he cried out.

"What's the matter?" Ella asked him.

Ethan felt around in his pockets some more. Still empty. "My gold coin! It's gone!"

"It's probably in your room," Ella said.

"No. I know I had it when we went

downtown yesterday. I was wearing this exact same hoodie," Ethan said worriedly.

Grandpa Harry leaned across the table. "Sounds like a mystery to me," he said with a twinkle in his eye.

"A mystery? We don't have *time* for a mystery," Ethan complained.

"Of course you do. Why don't you give me your to-do list, and I'll start tackling it. While I'm doing that, the two of you can look for the gold coin," Grandpa Harry offered.

With that, he took the list from the twins. He pulled his glasses out of

his jacket pocket and headed for the stairs, humming to himself.

Ethan turned to Ella. *"Now* what? I just want my coin back!"

"Okay, let's think. We spent the whole day yesterday running errands with Dad. Maybe you dropped it along the way," Ella suggested.

"*Great.* It could be anywhere!" Ethan wailed.

Ella's brown eyes lit up. "Not *anywhere.*"

She reached for her new journal and a pen. She opened it up to the first page and began to write. "Let's see. Yesterday, we went to the bakery first," she said. "Then the bead store, then

the bookstore, then the comic-book store."

"What are you doing?" Ethan asked.

"You mean, what are *we* doing? *We* are going to retrace our steps from yesterday and find your gold coin!" Ella said excitedly.

CHAPTER 5

And the Search Begins

"First stop: Petunia Bakery," Ella announced.

A tiny bell jingled as she and Ethan opened the door. Inside the shop, the smell of freshly baked cookies made their mouths water.

The bakery and the rest of downtown Brookeston were only a few blocks from the Briars' house. With

Mrs. Briar at the mall and Mr. Briar busy cleaning, it had been easy for the twins to sneak away. Grandpa Harry had wished them luck and gone back to taping up boxes as the twins left.

Mrs. Valentine, the baker, waved at them from behind the cash register. As always, the glass counter was filled

with cupcakes, pies, and lots of other yummy-looking treats.

"I thought you'd left for your trip," she called out.

"We're leaving at three o'clock," Ella replied.

Then Mrs. Valentine held out two chocolate-chip cookies. "How about a

cookie on the house as a *bon voyage* present?"

The twins were at the counter in about two seconds flat. As Ella bit into the delicious cookie, she opened up her journal. "Mrs. Valentine, when we were here yesterday, Ethan may have dropped a gold coin. Have you seen it?" she asked.

"It has a globe on one side and a hawk on the other," Ethan told the baker.

"No, I haven't seen anything like that. Let me check in the lost-and-found box." Mrs. Valentine dipped her head behind the counter and rummaged around.

While Mrs. Valentine was busy, Ella and Ethan searched the rest of the shop. They peered under tables and chairs. They scanned tall shelves packed with jams, jellies, and teas. They looked through the window display.

By the time they were done, Ethan had found a couple of pennies and Ella had found a rhine-stone hairpin—but no gold coin.

They brought the hairpin up to Mrs. Valentine.

"Goodness, I've been looking for that everywhere!" she exclaimed. "Sometimes you think you've lost something forever. But it turns out, it's right under your nose! Thank you so much, children!"

"You're welcome!" Ella said.

"I'm afraid your coin isn't in my lost-and-found box," Mrs. Valentine apologized. "But I will e-mail your parents if I come across it."

Ella and Ethan thanked the baker and said good-bye. Before they left, Ella opened up her journal and jotted down some notes:

We didn't find the gold coin at Petunia Bakery.

We did find Mrs. Valentine's hairpin, though.

She said: "Sometimes you think you've lost something forever. But it turns out, it's right under your nose."

CHAPTER 6

Best Friends and a Soccer Ball

Ethan and Ella headed over to Bead Mania next. It was Ella's favorite store in Brookeston. Ethan had no idea why. Who cared about making bracelets and stuff, anyway?

"Um, maybe you should go inside alone," Ethan suggested. "I'll search the perimeter. You know, that means the outside part," he added quickly.

"I know what 'perimeter' means," Ella snapped. "Fine, then. I'll just go inside and investigate by myself. 'Investigate' means look around."

"I *know* that," Ethan said, rolling his eyes.

Ella headed into the store. Ethan decided to start with the flower garden in front. He got down on his knees and squinted at the dirt beneath the plants. He wished he had a metal detector. He saw an ant, a worm, and a ladybug—but no coin.

"Hey! Ethan!"

Ethan glanced up. His best friend, Theo, stood on the sidewalk, holding a soccer ball.

The two boys had said good-bye to each other on Friday after their game against the Fall Creek Falcons. Still, it was nice to run into Theo one last time.

"Hi!" Ethan rose to his feet. "Is there a game today?"

"Nah. I went to the park to kick the ball around. Nobody was there, though." Theo looked away.

Ethan felt bad. He and Theo often went to that park together to play soccer on the weekends.

"So what are you doing?" Theo pointed to the flower garden.

"I'm looking for my gold coin. My grandpa gave it to me as a going-away present. But I dropped it somewhere yesterday," Ethan explained.

"Wow! Is there anything I can do to help? What does it look like?" Theo asked.

"Well . . . it's about the size of a quarter. It has a globe on one side and a hawk on the other," Ethan replied.

Theo thought for a moment. "I have a gold coin in my coin collection. It's an old train token. I actually thought it was a quarter. It doesn't have a

globe or a hawk on it, though."

Just then, Ella came out of Bead Mania.

"Sorry it took so long. I didn't find your coin." She turned to Theo. "Oh, hi! Are you here to buy some beads?"

"No way," Theo replied. "I'm on my way home. I have to study for that math test tomorrow."

"We'd better go, too," Ella said to

Ethan. "We still have two more stores on our list."

"Yeah," Ethan agreed. "Bye again," he said sadly.

"Bye, Eth," Theo replied.

BEADS!

S
F

Just then, Theo tossed his soccer ball at Ethan. Ethan returned it with a perfect header. Theo jumped up in the air and caught it neatly.

The two boys laughed and waved good-bye.

"I hope you find your coin!" Theo called out.

Ethan hoped so, too. *Soon.*

CHAPTER 7
A Little Bit of Luck?

Ella and Ethan's next stop was the Wise Owl bookstore.

"I guess you two didn't buy enough books when you were here with your dad yesterday," Mr. DeMarco joked when the twins walked in.

On Saturday, Ella, Ethan, and their dad had picked up some books for the trip. Ella had selected *The Secret Garden*.

Ethan had chosen *The Borrowers*.

"Actually, we are here to solve a mystery," Ella told Mr. DeMarco.

Mr. DeMarco pushed his glasses up on his nose. "A mystery? You mean like something from a Nancy Drew or Hardy Boys story?"

"Exactly!" Ella said. "Ethan's gold

coin disappeared yesterday, so we're retracing our steps."

"I may have dropped it here," Ethan added.

"A gold coin? Hmm . . . I don't think I've seen one of those lately," Mr. DeMarco said. "But let me look in my cash register. Maybe it got mixed in with the other coins somehow."

"Is it okay if we look around for it?"
Ethan asked.

"Of course! Take all the time you
need," Mr. DeMarco replied.

Ella and Ethan agreed to split up to
search for the coin. Ella would take the
kids' books room, and Ethan would
take the main room.

Once she was in the kids' room, Ella searched everywhere. But there was no sign of Ethan's coin.

A girl with red braids wandered into the room. Her face was buried in a book.

"Hannah?" Ella called out.

The girl glanced up. It *was* Hannah!

"*Ella!*" Hannah exclaimed.

The two girls rushed up to each other and hugged.

"What are you doing here?" cried Hannah. "I thought you were gone!"

"We're leaving this afternoon," Ella told her.

Hannah sighed. "I'm going to miss you so much! What's going to happen to our book club? And our poetry club?" She and Ella were always coming up with fun clubs for just the two of them.

"Well, we can e-mail our poems to each other. And we can e-mail about the books we read, too," Ella said.

Hannah nodded eagerly. "Yes! And you have to tell me about all the places you visit. And send lots of photos, too. I am *so* jealous!"

"You are?" Ella asked, surprised.

Hannah nodded. "You're taking a trip around the world. You're the

luckiest person I know!" she exclaimed.

The girls exchanged one last hug before Hannah left to meet up with her mom. Ella took a minute to sit down on a beanbag chair and write in her journal.

I ran into Hannah at the
bookstore. I'll miss her a lot.
  She says I'm really lucky to be
going on a trip around the world.
  I'm starting to wonder if maybe

I am . . .

Just then, Ethan rushed into the kids' room.

"Hey, Ella! Guess what?" he said excitedly.

CHAPTER 8

A Bright Idea

"Did you find your coin?" Ella asked her brother.

Ethan shook his head. "No, but I just thought of something! Theo told me he added a train token to his coin collection by accident because he thought it was a quarter."

"So?" Ella responded.

"So what if someone found my coin

and didn't look at it carefully? Maybe they thought it was a quarter, too," Ethan said.

"That's a good idea," Ella replied.

The twins said good-bye again to Mr. DeMarco and left the store. They made a quick stop at Galaxy Comics next door, just to make sure the gold coin wasn't there. It wasn't—although the storeowner, Mr. Max, gave Ethan a new comic book as a *bon voyage* present.

Ethan glanced at his watch as they left the comic-book store. The twins had less than half an hour to find the coin and get home.

They turned the corner and found themselves in the town square. It was a sunny spring day, and everyone seemed to be out. On one side of the big fountain, a man played jazz music on his saxophone. People stopped by to listen. They tossed coins into his

open saxophone case.

Coins . . .

"Ella!" Ethan said in a low voice. "What if someone found my coin and gave it to the saxophone player?"

Ella's eyes widened. "Let's go check it out!"

The twins rushed over to the musi-cian. They squeezed through the crowd to get closer to the case.

Ethan bent down. No gold coin.

The musician looked over at Ethan suspiciously. Did he think Ethan was a thief?

"My coin's not in there. Let's keep looking," Ethan whispered to Ella.

"Hey, Ethan? I've been thinking about something Mrs. Valentine said," Ella remarked as they walked away. She pulled out her journal and opened it to the second page. She pointed to what she had written.

"'Sometimes you think you've lost something forever. But it turns out, it's right under your nose,'" Ethan read.

He thought about this. "What does 'under your nose' mean?"

"It means that something you've lost might be closer than you think," Ella told him. "Maybe your coin is right under our noses, and we just don't know it."

"Ethan! Ella!"

Their neighbor Mrs. Sanchez waved to them from a bench. Her dog, Sugarplum, bounded up to the twins, wagging her tail. Ethan and Ella had known Sugarplum since she was a puppy.

"Hi, Mrs. Sanchez! Hi, Sugarplum!" Ethan said as the twins joined Mrs. Sanchez on the bench.

"Are you here to make a wish before you leave for your trip?" Mrs. Sanchez asked.

"Huh?" Ethan asked, puzzled.

"At the fountain," Mrs. Sanchez said with a chuckle. "The two of you have been throwing pennies and making wishes since you were old enough to walk. Why, I remember—"

"Ella, that's it!" Ethan practically shouted. "It's right under our noses!"

Ella glanced around wildly. "It is? Where?"

"What are you two talking about?" Mrs. Sanchez asked, confused.

"We'll explain later. Come on, Ella!"

Ethan jumped to his feet and began weaving through the crowd.

Ella followed. "Where are we going now?" she asked her brother.

"To the fountain!" Ethan cried.

When they reached the fountain, Ethan leaned over and peered inside. He circled it once, twice, three times.

There were hundreds of coins lying on the bottom. The water glittered like a quilt of silver and copper.

Ethan swished his hand through the cool water. He saw pennies, nickels, dimes, and quarters—but no gold coins.

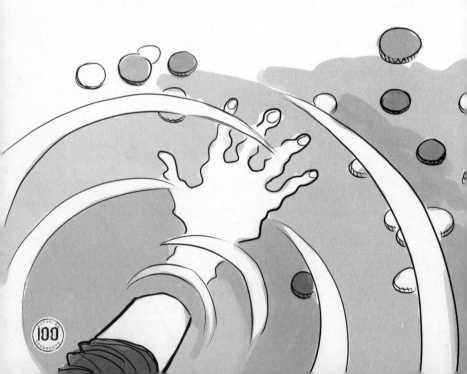

"I don't think we're allowed to do that," Ella said nervously.

"Just trust me," Ethan replied.

A church bell tolled in the distance. Ethan glanced at his watch again. It was 2:45. They had to get home or they'd miss their flight!

A cloud passed over the sun. Suddenly a shimmer of gold caught Ethan's eye.

"A gold coin!" Ethan cried out.

He reached into the fountain. He pulled out the coin and studied it closely.

On one side was a globe . . . and on the other was a hawk. It was his coin!

He grinned and showed it to Ella.

The twins high-fived each other. Mystery solved!

CHAPTER 9

The Last Good-bye

Ella and Ethan got home just as their mom's car pulled into the driveway.

Mrs. Briar emerged with an armful of shopping bags. "I'm sorry that took so long," she apologized.

The twins exchanged a glance. Mrs. Briar obviously had no idea that they'd been gone for the past few hours.

"Oh, that's okay, Mom," Ella said, trying to catch her breath.

"Yeah, Mom. No problem," Ethan added.

Mrs. Briar gave them a suspicious look. "Did you get everything done on your list? Please tell me you did."

"Um . . . ," Ethan and Ella began.

"*Sure* they did!"

Grandpa Harry stepped through the front door holding a cardboard box. "Come have some lemonade before you leave!" he called out cheerfully.

Mr. Briar came outside, too. His face and hands were smudged with dirt.

"Hi, Jo. Hey, kids! Sorry I couldn't help with your list. The basement cleanup took longer than I thought."

"Andy, you're a mess! Why, we're going to have to do a cleanup on *you*," Mrs. Briar joked.

Mr. and Mrs. Briar went inside the

house. Ella and Ethan rushed up to Grandpa Harry with big smiles on their faces.

Ethan opened his fist and showed Grandpa Harry the gold coin.

"I knew you two could do it," Grandpa Harry said with a wink.

* * *

The taxi was early. It sat in the driveway while Ethan, Ella, and their parents scrambled around the house to make sure they had everything.

"You're ready. You've got everything. Now, *go!*" Grandpa Harry ordered the four of them not much later. "I'll do a last sweep after you're gone."

"All right." Mrs. Briar gave him a hug. "I'll e-mail you as soon as we get there."

"*Bon voyage*, JoJo," said Grandpa Harry.

Mrs. Briar brushed back a tear. "Thanks, Dad. Love you!"

Ethan and Ella stood frozen in their spots. Grandpa Harry leaned down and patted them on their heads.

"I don't want to say good-bye," Ella said, choking back a sob.

"I don't want to say good-bye, either." Ethan sniffled.

"Then let's say *arrivederci* instead," Grandpa Harry suggested.

"What does that mean?" the twins asked.

"It's Italian for 'see you again,'" their grandfather explained.

A few minutes later, the family piled into the taxi. As it pulled out of the driveway, Ella and Ethan turned around in their seats.

Grandpa Harry stood on the lawn,

waving. The twins waved back.

"*Arrivederci*," they whispered.

They kept waving until they couldn't see Grandpa Harry anymore.

Ella clutched her journal.

Ethan held his gold coin tightly.

After all that, both Ella and Ethan really were excited about the big new adventure that was about to unfold. They had sights to see . . . people to meet . . . and, maybe, just maybe, more mysteries to solve.

GLOSSARY

God morgon (Swedish) = Good morning

Bon voyage (French) = Have a good trip

Arrivederci (Italian) = See you again

CHECK OUT THE NEXT

GREETINGS FROM SOMEWHERE

ADVENTURE!

VENICE, ITALY

Ella Briar and her twin brother, Ethan, had never been to Venice, Italy, before. They'd never been to a floating city, either!

Venice was made up of a bunch of tiny islands connected by canals and bridges. Some people were using boats to get around, and others were walking over the bridges from one street to another.

"Here's our hotel!" the twins' mother, Josephine Briar, said brightly.

Pink, yellow, and pale green buildings lined both sides of the canal. Pretty flowers and vines filled the window boxes. There were no cars or bicycles on the cobblestone streets, only people walking.

For a moment, Ella and Ethan were so shocked by their surroundings that they forgot they were supposed to be sad. Or mad. Or sad and mad.

Just yesterday, they had said good-bye to everything and everyone they loved. Their mom was starting her new job as a travel writer. That meant she had to travel to different foreign cities and write about them for her newspaper column, "Journeys with Jo"!

The Briars entered the hotel. A woman greeted them from the front desk.

"*Buon giorno!*" she called.

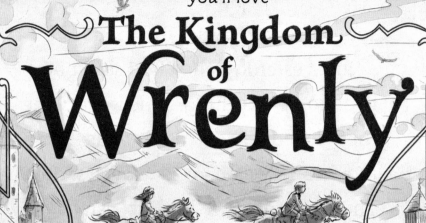
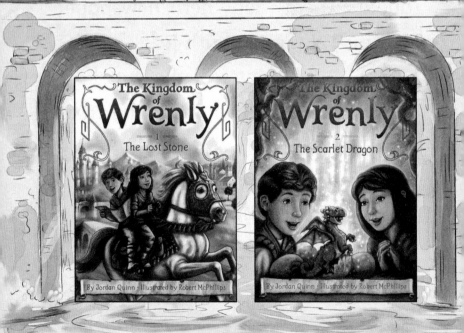